WIZARD'S LAST RULE

Kathryn May Howard Whitaker

Copyright © 2017 Jerry Whitaker
All rights reserved
First Edition

PAGE PUBLISHING, INC.
New York, NY

First originally published by Page Publishing, Inc. 2017

ISBN 978-1-64082-154-5 (Hardcover)
ISBN 978-1-64082-153-8 (Digital)

Printed in the United States of America

WIZARD'S LAST RULE

To my family and their own kind and encouraging magic.

Wizard's Last Rule

written and Illustrated by Kathryn Whitaker

It sounded like thunder banging and booming. There stood the witch. One hand on her broom, her other hand worked hurling spell after spell that sizzled and sparked, each one missing the wizard by more than a mark. Like fireflies, her magic simply blinked out. She needed more power. She knew that to be true—oh, but what was a poor witch to do? She meant to rule Elderwood Forest with her goblins and friends. First she must be rid of Galvin McVien. Then a demon offered her aid. He too wanted Elderwood; he'd take it in trade... "For a tiny cave in Elderwood Forest, that's all," he wrung his hands in glee, "and I would be paid!" In this den that led to the underworld, his home would then be made.

The wizard was wizened and tattered with age. Still he was the strongest magic. "No, Lena," he yelled. "Take your demon and yourself. Leave these righteous woods, there is no room!" Then he sent her flying on gales of wind passing the moon, back to Witchland, riding her broom. Now the wizard was old and needed to leave Elderwood Forest. He was tired, in need of restoring rest, so he'd walk through the mist. But first he'd banish Witch Lena that was top on his list. Forever banished, never to be seen, her magic dark evil and mean.

Witch Lena stroked her thin, pointy chin and reached for her familiar spirit helper, a talking cat named Grim, with supernatural power.

"What do you think, Grim, my pet? Are the goblins right? Did the old wizard really leave Elderwood Forest, as my goblins are whispering?"

"No, it's a trap!" was all Grim would say.

"Pooh! You're just being your old skeptical self."

"No, it's a trap," Grim said, licking his paw.

"Listen, I hear the goblins again."

"The wizard is gone from the forest this night. We watched Mistress Witch. He put his magic book in the nook of a very old tree."

"If it's true . . . I must have that book. I could reverse Wizard Galvin's spell that keeps me from Elderwood Forest."

Lena's silken robe swished softly. She turned to her magic mirror, her voice low and thoughtful. "Magic mirror, find my goblin, do make him appear."

A vision curled into a view, a sniveling goblin trying to stand very still.

"Ah, Gole'o, take me to this book!"

"Yes, Mistress Witch," he whined, "it's over the hill."

Through tangles of fallen limbs leaves and such, he ran just as fast as his little leg would go, stopped, then pointed his shaking hand to a large oak tree all shining with gold.

"It's there in the tr-tree, Mistress Witch, I . . . I cannot touch," he stammered in a terrified voice.

He knew the witch did terrible things to any who disobeyed, taking their tongues—and other things! He held his mouth tight.

"Take your fingers out of your mouth, my dear, you'll speak clearer."

The goblin shut his mouth, not saying another word.

"Humph, the wizard thinks himself so clever, hiding his book with magic gold. Gole'o, bring the goblins to Witchland," she said, dismissing the goblin with a wave of her powerful land.

Climbing over the knolls and hollows, through a forest all damp with dew, a shaky goblin ran; he almost flew.

Witch Lena exhaled. She needed the oracle to tell her what to do! Her ancient book of shadows handed down from the great grand witch of all would have the spell she had in mind.

"This spell will work quite nicely."

She chanted arcane words of magic then opened each vial of dark, nasty things—herbs of power and other unnameable things, carefully following the spell precisely—finishing her potion with a bit of rotten entrails, a pinch of eye of newt, and a handful of snails. All this she added to her cook pot—wet, steaming, bubbling elixir paired tendrils of vapors that rose through the air, creating a wraithlike specter. The incantation transformed the ghostly apparition.

"A she-banshee—how wonderful—do come to me, come closer to Lena," coached the witch. "Now, let me see. Why, you've never looked lovelier."

Breathy word graded across a firelit room—her voice hollow like its tomb.

"You have summoned me, Mistress Witch?"

"Yes, indeed, my pet. I have an errand only you can do best," the witch crackled. "I shall place my magical cape around you. Endowed with my magic, you will be my instrument. You may go to Eldewood Forest, where I cannot, and get what I most definitely need. Now, shoo, fly into the forest, let my magic guide you to the book. Bring it to me at all costs, let nothing stop you."

"Yes, Mistress Witch," agreed the banshee, "I'll not get lost."

old filtered down in front of the tree.
"Oh, my, is this really gold? I'll be needing my pot, there is too much to hold."

So being a leprechaun, he just reached in and took . . . But what . . . All he got was a book? He hesitated.

"Okay, where's my gold?" he said, looking around, scratching his head. "It's gone?"

Then he spied with dread . . . swopping down at him from the sky, a banshee wrapped in a black cape.

"No!" Mac Flin yelled. "This wee book is mine! It's not yours to take!"

But the caped banshee hugged the magical tome.

"It belongs to the witch!" her ghostly voice boomed, and she tugged all the harder.

Mac Flin held on tight to his new book, using all his might.

Rrrip! Right down the middle, the magic book split.

The she-banshee flew off his peal of laughter, knowing she had gotten what she had come after. The witch's own powerful magic held the volume that nestled tightly in the folds of her black, silky cape.

On the leaves-scattered ground, Mac Flin sat down, his back against the gnarly tree. His gold had been stolen and now half his book too.

"Sure, that banshee was demon was sent! Whatever did the she-banshee mean, when it screamed, 'It's the witch's book'?" he grumbled, thumbing through the pages. "Looks to me this book belongs to magic.
"The elves will be knowing these rhymes. As for me, I've no more time."

He tucked the packet into his jacket, turned to the tree, dropped down on the knee, and tipped his hat—knowing it was magic-sent. Then he quietly slipped through the forest bright with filtered sunlight.

Lena was thrilled. At last she'd bring the trolls from the hills and her goblins from their holes—even the giants would come—once she was mistress of Elderwood. Already she had captured a few more fairies, with her magic flower that put them to sleep—their body lights burning bright under glass domes. And soon she would discover what made them glow.

Then the banshee was there.

"My job is complete, release me back to my grave," stated the she-banshee, swaying.

Witch Lena scowled as she gazed at what lay in the palm of her hands, her voice icy-calm.

"The other half of my book . . . is now in the hands of a leprechaun? Return to the forest. Find that thing who wears the green! Get the rest of my book!" she shrilled. "Let no one stop you, bring them to me if they try! Most of all, find me that crook!"

The leprechaun became visible, looking back over his shoulder as he tramped through hemlock, black walnut, and maple leaves.

"Welcome Mac Flin," a beaming elf stood there, seeming to appear right from thin air, as only the elves could do.

Mac Flin faced Eppen, the leader of the small band of elves of Elderwood Forest.

"Where's everyone?" he inquired, looking around.

Trell and Elfin dropped to the mushroom-studded ground.

"A bit jumpy for a leprechaun," Jam chuckled.

"Aye, laddies, I've brought a book of strange magic, it was in the nook of a magical tree."

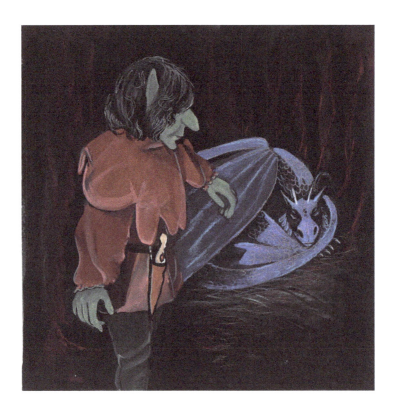

Onton glanced at Dracolleen.

"Sleep on, my dragon queen."

He had raised the dragon from a hatching dragon egg he found abandoned in a cave—much like himself, orphaned at a tender age. Onton was taken in a troll raid. The hungry troll held him to his long, running nose, in a thick-knotted hand.

"And what is your name, little dark elf?" the big troll asked while sniffing him.

"Onton is my name!" the little elf said defiantly.

"Well, Onton, you'll be a very tasty snack," replied the monster. "But you're so small! Yuck, you're not even a bite . . . but you'll do," he growled through fat, drooling lips, lifting his hairless head. He opened his smelly mouth and fell over dead.

Hidden elves in a giant elm tree shot their magic bolts, right through its thick, yellow hide, killing that troll. The elves took Onton in as one of their own. A tiny elf child was clad only in ragged threadbare clothes and an amulet held by a silver chain around his neck, a charm of silver magic—a magic of mystery no one knew how to unlock.

Onton heard the familiar voice of the leprechaun, but this time, Mac Flin's voice rang with fear.

"Sleep on, my lady," he whispered to his dragon.

Then he climbed from their home under the dome of a hollowed root of the gnarled oak tree. He scrambled onto a branch, while clusters of green acorns and leaves kept him from sight. He heard the leprechaun explain his encounter with the black-caped banshee and book of magic.

"Sounds like trouble brewing," the dark elf said with a frown, silently sliding down the tree.

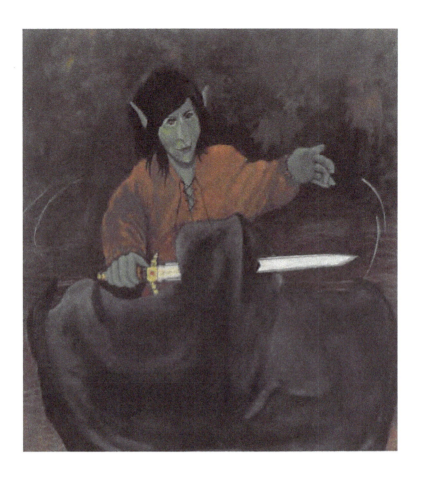

Only to face the swaying black-caped banshee.
"Your Mac Flin's black cape, you'll not pass me," he stated, raising his sword.

"Leprechaun," the raspy voice came from the hollow depth of the empty cape.

The dark elf slashed the black cape, without knowing it was really the witch's magic he had just struck down.

"Let's dance," he challenged.

Suddenly, the crumpled cloak sprang up with a twang. In a quick, spiral curl, the cape banshee twirled, encircling, wrapping the trapped elf.

Silently, together they flew into the forest. With Onton in his dark cocoon, the banshee hummed her ghostly tune.

"**M**other of all fairies, did you see? Did you see inside that cape?" Trell yelled. "Spidery webbed hair flowing, howling through fanged teeth in a mouth that wasn't there, we've a banshee in our mist!"

"On be golly! That's what I've been trying to tell you," Mac began. "And now," he stopped, buried his face in his hands, "I'm the one that brought that ghostly thing into our midst. Mother of all fairies, I'm so sorry, she's taken Onton away."

"Easy, old friend," Eppen said, laying a comforting hand on the leprechaun's shoulder. "You're not the one to blame. There's dark magic in play, that she-banshee's a spirit from the grave. This one has power that's not her own. You've told us about this witch's book—well, there's only one witch in these parts . . . Lena. Witch Lena's behind this, I'll bet my buckles on it. I think Onton was trying to help. He just got in the way."

"Yeah, he saved my hide, I'm thinking," the leprechaun said, wiping his eyes, then held up the book. "I'm thinkin' this is what it was really after."

"This book is magical, but to what purpose? Its meaning is concealed, pressed tightly between these pages," Trell said.

They all agreed.

Dracolleen the dragon had followed the dark elf from their underground home. He saw the cape slide over Onton and was bewildered and didn't comprehend why it flew off, taking her friend. She tasted evil's lingering share; her nostrils flared. Her breath became a fiery bane of scouring flames, which sent crackling, popping sparks, scoring high into treetops.

The forest fairies of Elderwood hid, whispering, "Beware, beware."

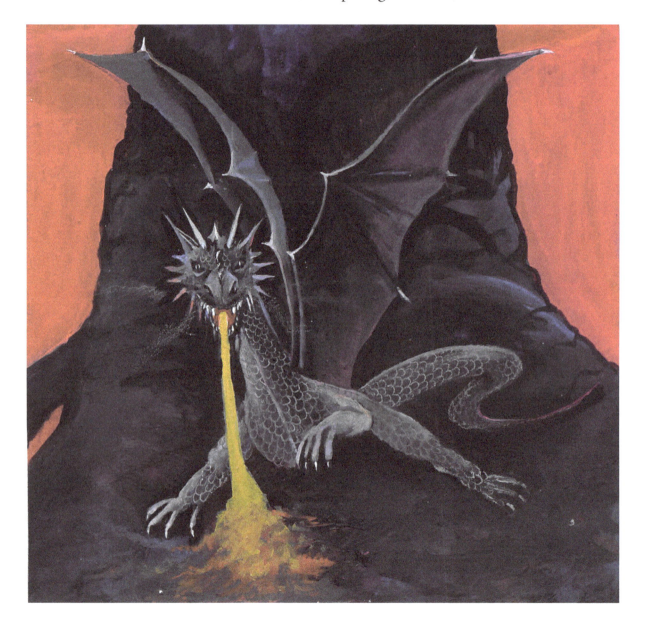

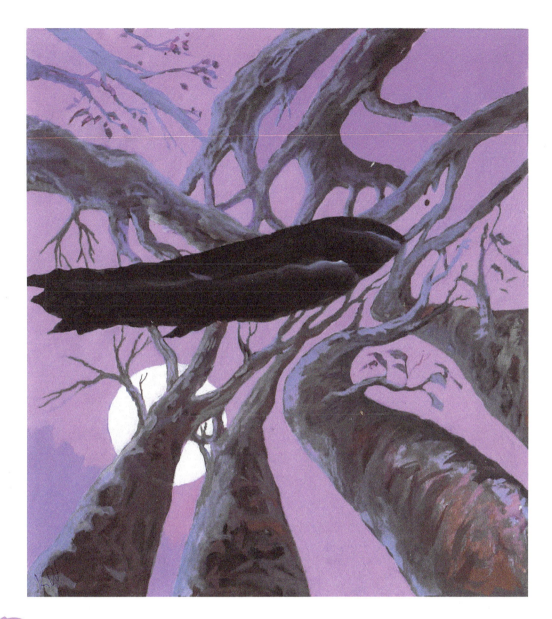

nton used all his strength trying to stop the flying cape he was hopelessly caught in. He tried reaching out, but he could not.

"The witch wants you," hissed the banshee, "so we shall fly."

They spirited through tunnels of low branches. Onton's thoughts were of Dracolleen and last chances. He hadn't even said goodbye. Bent limbs reached out, trying to reach him, but they could not.

It looked bad for their friend. Fearing his fate, they embarked the very night on an adventure that would hopefully lead them to Witchland. A silvered moon showed fractions of prism light, enough for their elven sight to guide them easily through the night forest. Erie screeches greeted them as they entered Dreadwood, an old forest known for its wild magic.

Snapping twigs alerted the travelers; they were not alone.

"It's a good place for an ambush," Eppen said, raising his hand, holding back his small band. "We're following goblins, I'd say, see the tracks?"

"Yeah," Elfin growled, "I can smell a waylay."

"They're lurking behind those trees. Ready your weapons," Eppen ordered. "Watch your back!"

"The witch calls them," Jam remarked dryly, "will hang 'em in their rucksacks."

"Good enough," Trell whispered, holding back a smirk, sliding behind mossy boulders.

"Careful, elf boy," said a voice.

Startled, Trell looked up, and atop the boulder, a tiny fairy called to him. A brilliance shone around her.

"With your eye, follow me, elf boy."

Trell watched her slip along a forest floor of root mass and wild grasses, with mushrooms and pine needles, leaves. Then up through pine boughs, her firelights blinked on and off, showing the dark silhouettes of goblins all hunkered down, hiding behind the tresses of leaves and branches.

A bright, glowing fairy light revealed to Mac Flin the leprechaun where the goblins were hidden.

"Ah, the good fairy has sent us her wee sprite," he whispered to Eppen, winked, then became invisible.

"Be ready, old friend, the witch is up to no good, but it seems we've got help," Mac Flin the leprechaun said, as his ghostly voice floated across the crisp, pine-scented air.

He crept silently, coming up behind a score of goblins armed with their deadly weapons—spears, spiked clubs, and long knives ready.

The leprechaun shimmied up a tall willow tree, right on top of the goblins. He reached over its long branch, waving the spell book slowly back and forth.

In his best witch voice, he hissed, "F<small>LEE, YOU FOOLS, DANGER, FLEE</small>!"

Well, the goblins—hearing the mistress and seeing the spell book just floating, and being her groveling, terrified minions—they attempted, in their obedience to her, to frantically leave their site of the ambush.

Bumping, shoving, and climbing over each other, swarms of goblins finally managed to run away from the elves into the forest. All but four.

The goblins charged, yelling their war chant, swinging spiked clubs high overhead.

Twang, thud was all they heard when elven bolts slammed into, them biting deeply.

"I'm guessing we'll not be spending the rest of this glorious night with all these inhospitable folks running loose," Mac Flin chuckled.

"Your little trick bought us some time, leprechaun," Elfin snarled, "but I'll not rest easy until this nasty business is over."

Gray fog covered the ghostly pathways, as five weary companions continued their quest, traveling deeper into Dreadwood Forest. The cloudy mist settled heaviest over the dark, tangled forest flooring. Silently, the elves crept along, following one another closely, through the damp darkness. Slurping, plopping sound—like thick porridge cooking—followed them; and now it crawled closer, covering the ground. When last in line, and the first to sink under the bubbling, slimy mud—Jam turned back around. Then Elfin, who was next to him, called out sharply. He was the second to pass out of sight, slipping down into the soggy, muddy ground.

"Stop," Eppen swung his arm out, saving Jam from the creeping, sucking mud by pulling him back around and away from the edge.

"Trell . . . Elfin," both Jam and Eppen called out.

"I cannot see him," Elfin answered from the pond of sucking mud.

"I fear he's gone under, and I'll not be lasting long either!" he tried to shout.

But they were not alone! Fairies of Elderwood Forest heard the banshee's evil drone. They saw through the cape's allusion, to the dark magic of Witch Lena, the evil crone. How she had gotten through wizard Galvin's magic banishing spell was unbeknownst. The fairies sent their magic warning. It spiraled throughout the forest, telling all the diminutive beings that an evil witch was once again in their forest dwelling.

Eppen and Jam reached for a log that was stuck in the forest debris. Mac Flin the leprechaun tied his rope to a nearby tree then ran to the edge of the sucking mud, but he found his rope was too short.

"Hang on, Elfin! Jam and Eppen are getting a branch," Mac Flin yelled frantically, feeling helpless as he watched Elfin's struggle to stay afloat.

Shining like beacons of lights, wispy fairies appeared, carrying a long, thin twig between them. Their voices rang clear with a musical note as they laid the small twig on top of the mud. They clasped each other's hands in a magical trance, slowly circling in a mystical dance, and the tiny stick began to bud.

Suddenly, the small twig began to grow into a large branch, as big as a tree. A fairy flew in with a light, shiny rope. The tiny fairy looped one and around the thick branch, the other end over Elfin's wet and muddy head. Elfin pulled one arm up through the rope and held on tight.

And he called out, "I thank thee."

Another fairy shot under the mud with a shiny rope in tow. She materialized, hauling Trell up with her rope around his waist, up through the thick slime, barely in time.

The fairy handed the other end of the rope to the Jam and Mac Flin the leprechaun.

Trell's eyes were closed. He hung limp in the rope that was all aglow.

"Hey, elf boy, wake up," she whispered then softly brushed his face.

The slimy mud magically disappeared from his face. She leaned over and kissed him.

Trell's eye fluttered open. "You're a beautiful gem," he breathed with sigh.

"Ah, elf boy, again you seem to be in trouble."

"You've my thanks, lady of the light," Trell said quietly.

The elves hauled their friends off to safety.

"Beware of the creeping, hungry mud, it never stays put very long," the fairies sang. "You must release the fairies from the witch, she holds them captive in Witchland."
And then, just like that, the fairies were gone!
"Hey, elf boy, I think the pretty fairy in red is sweet on you," Elfin teased.
Trell said nothing, but his cheeks turned a pretty pink.

Leaving the crawling mud behind, the companions trekked the damp wooded lowland that led to a path of moss-covered rocks. A fairy ring of poison pie mushrooms squatted in a circle, protected near a clump of wild raspberries. The elves and leprechaun needed to find a canyon called Brock—a deep gorge that separated Dreadwood from Witchland. Somehow they had to cross, to get to witch Lena's fortress, where the banshee had taken Onton, trapped and held tight in her ghostly hand.

"Bah," Eppen moaned, "I think we've found our deep ravine, it's filled with biting thorns."

"Listen," Trell said, "there's running water, and I'm for a cool drink before finding our way through this brier storm."

Mac Flin opened his hand. A magic globe of light appeared, shimmering off a clear, running stream.

"When you're right, you're right," Mac Flin chuckled and beamed.

With their water skins filled, their thirst quenched, the five companions fell into a deep sleep, filled with colorful dreams of swimming wild and free . . .

Asleep brought on by magic! The sparkling stream the friends drank from—Soul Drinker was her name. Whosoever taster her magical waters would sleep . . . then shrink to the smallest molecule. In a chemical reaction, they would then join the sparkling stream running always free.

Fairies flew in, dusting the slumbering friends with their powerful magic—just in the nick of time, stopping the shrinking Soul Drinker from going any further . . .

Mac Flin the leprechaun shrieked when he opened his bleary green eyes, crawled to the edge of the boulder . . . looked over, and silently mouthed, "Suren me eyes lie!"

And the fairies kept a watchful eye on the leprechaun—their glowing bodies a rainbow prism, glowing in a bright octagon.

Then Mac Filn shouted, "Hey! . . . Where's everybody? . . . Anybody one out there? . . . Answer me!"

He opened his mouth to call again, but all that came out was a big yawn.

Trell, shaking his head in disbelief, stood up in grass tall as him, green and willowy.

Jam gulped as he slipped past something dark and squirmy, with a big mouth that puffed out billowy.

Elfin and Eppen awoke, hearing the leprechaun calling. Then Trell yelled as he climbed the leprechaun's rope, "Dreadwood's wild magic must have shrunk us!"

"That or the witch of Witchland," Elfin answered sarcastically. "We have to get out of this haunted forest."

Eppen frowned, "That my very well may be, but now we have a bigger problem! He pointed toward the forest. "And it's coming right toward us!"

"Me thirsty!" "Me hungry!" groaned two goblins as they tramped toward the witch's fortress in Withcland, passing the tiny elven companions.

Then the dark, squirmy bug shot something powdery out of his billowy mouth, which landed on Jam and started him sneezing in a uncontrollable fit. He couldn't hide or run, just stood there sneezing in front of two goblins—which caught the not-so-clever goblin's attention. All at once, the goblin swung back around, squatted down with a quizzical look.

Mac Flin became invisible; the other companions lay hidden; but Jan went on sneezing.

"Hey! A tiny elf!" the goblin chuckled. "Hum, I'll just squish you like a bug," he poked at Jam. "Hum! I wonder what an elf tastes like? Maybe good nibbles!" smacked the goblin as he licked his sharp pointy teeth.

And Jan sneezed on. He tried to run but still couldn't; he guessed his goose was cooked.

The goblin lifted the sneezing elf by the back of his shirt, opened his mouth wide, ready to eat the tiny treat.

Jam almost fainted from the foul, smelly break. Its bad odor stopped his sneezing, but the sight and the closeness of a mouth full of sharp, yellow teeth turned his heart into a loud, thumping drum, and he wondered how much it was going to hurt.

Suddenly, the goblin dropped Jam.

"Bees bite me!" howled both goblins, dancing around, swatting at the tiny arrows protruding from their knees.

Jam hit the ground running hard, joining his waiting friends. With bows at the ready and still feathered, they fled the howling goblins, escaping into the dark woods. Jam felt like he'd been hit with a battering ram.

𝒮o our friends ran, into a jungle of corded roots, tangles of munchy twigs, toadstools, and leafy vines. It all became an ominous threat.

"How are we to save Onton and the fairy captives, when we can't even save ourselves from these hunted woods? We must have help, if we are to succeed," Eppen called with his arms raised to the magical powers of the land of In Between.

The friends rounded a decaying stump. A monster with fifteen legs, on both sides, its jaw full of subduing poison, writhed closer. The friends backed up as one; the monster inched closer.

"On the count of three, fall back and fan out," Eppen whispered back over his shoulder to Elfin.

"Is that our plan?" Elfin asked doubtingly.

"Yeah! Pass it back," Eppen reaffirmed. "One . . . two . . . three!"

All four fanned out, except Mac Flin. He stood his ground and now faced the monster all alone. It took his breath away—such a monster, he had never seen.

"What is that thing? What can it be?" the leprechaun asked.

Eppen grabbed the leprechaun's coat and pulled him back.

"*I AM CENTIPEEEDE, IF YOU PLEASE! AND IF YOU STOP YOUR CAT-TAH-WALLEN, AND JUST GO AROUND THE CORNER, THERE YOU'LL FIND YOUR STEED! NOW PLEEEASE LET ME EAT MY MEAL, AS YOU SEE IT AWAITS ME, IF YOU PLEASE!*"

The elves looked. Sure enough, a cockroach sat under a leaf; it seemed to be at ease.

    The rain came in huge, heavy droplets of translucent water, hitting five weary companions like falling stones. They sheltered under kin bolete mushrooms, with gingerbread-colored tops, and watched the pebbling rain play itself out. Then the companions crept with care, moving closer to Brock ravine, they hoped.

"Now what?" Trell yelled angrily, staggering back.

"What is it?" Eppen questioned.

"Didn't you all feel it? The ground just moved!"

A giant dragon head swung around, looking Trell right in the eye.

"Dracolleen," he gulped.

"Yes, it's me, your eyes see," she said, looking at each one and not seeing her friend, the dark elf. "Where's Onton?"

"The banshee took him to the witch in Witchland. We were on our way to rescue him," Eppen offered.

"You're so tiny, how can you bring Onton back to me? How did you get so small?"

"Dracolleen! You must be our steed the centipede told us we'd find."

"I do not understand you. Did your brain get addled when you became small?" the dragon ask.

"No, Dracolleen, but we have to get out of Dreadwood's forest! Will you fly us to the witch fortress?"

"Very well, I will fly, and we shall see that wicked banshee and evil witch."

"With your help, we may still rescue Onton, and we'll try to explain our size."

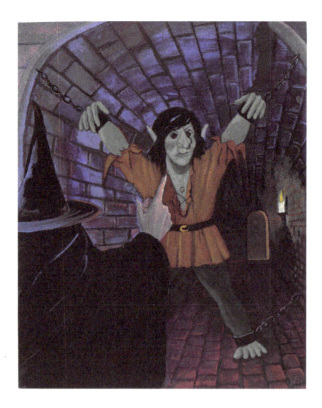

With a flip of Witch Lena's hand, irons chains appeared from the overhead arch, locking Onton's wrists and ankles.

"One moment," Witch Lena ordered the banshee. "This dark elf," she gave Onton a steady stare, "wants to tell me where the leprechaun is!"

Onton's only response was sly smile.

"Grim, my kitty, are you hungry?" Witch Lena sang.

The witch's familiar Grim began sharpening his long, pointy claws on an old cedar log. Onton began to worry.

"I think I can find a mouse for you, ooh," the witch sang. "Yes, a fine mouse with a long nose," she faced the dark elf, "just like yours, Onton! You'll want to talk to me, but you see, you'll not be able tooo . . ." Peals of witch laughter echoed around old stone walls . . . "Because you'll be a mouse."

Her words were magic. Grim her familiar began brushing and rubbing against her black, silky robe.

"SHIM-OREE LET ME SEE A HOUSE MOUSE IN FRONT OF MEEEE, TIMTIM—ADEE LET ME NOW SEE A MOUSE!"

Suddenly, Onton felt very odd. He looked down at his mouse foot. "Yuk" he squealed, "the witch has made me into a MOUSE!"

He scurried across the floor, hiding in the dusty shadows.

"Now where were we? . . . Kitty kitty, come to Lena."

Onton shivered in the dark. Then he saw white fangs gleaming, and a furry paw shot out.

Dracolleen sped through a cobalt sky—until a flying black cape caught her eye. She blasted her dragon fire, sent it searing across the sky, slamming right into the witch's cape. Her incinerating hot flames turned the cape to crispy ash that floated throughout the air. Like goose down it drifted over a tangled landscape.

"This time," Dracolleen murmured, "the banshee did not escape."

"I," screamed the banshee, "am no longer the witch's playful token."

Its magical hold over the now-disappearing she-banshee broken, the companions heard a distant whine, "Thank, you'ooz, I'm free'ee."

"Look," Elfin cried, pointing down through the mist, "scores of goblin on their way to Witchland, to do the witch's evil witchery."

There silhouetted in early morning, mist stood the witch's castle ever and tall, with her darkened tower standing spear-point sharp. Five companions and one dragon found the rampart, with its broad stone top and defendable wall. There Darcolleen could sit down unexposed, in this castle that appeared so diabolical.

"It's a creepy place, all right," Mac Flin shouted back. "No doubt will have ourselves a time finding Onton in this maze of roundabout. I'm not sure what's more scary, witch or castle?"

The elves and leprechaun climbed off the dragon, landing on the ledge of the rampart.

"Thank you, Dracolleen, we'll be coming out as soon as our business is complete, one way or another," Eppen said.

"Be careful, Dracolleen, no tellin' what's lurking around this menacing place, and watch for traps!" Eppen cautioned the dragon.

Then the companions quietly slipped over the wall. The dragon flew off, having her own plans to attend to.

T he friends put their ropes away, along with their magic collapsible bows that fit alongside their quivers, full of deadly bolts. Opting for the spider's thread that hung in cling ropes along the wall, one by one the companions dropped over the edge on borrowed spider's thread, hoping not to meet the web's dark mistress.

"Hurry, lads," Mac Flin yelled, "we've woken the web mistress. I don't think the black widow liked us using her web ladders..."

The elves and leprechaun kept to the concealing shadow, pulling back when they spotted a black cat, with its paw planted firmly on top of a mouse tail. The mouse squirmed frantically, trying to escape its tormentor; it was touch and go. With lightning speed, the cat slapped its other paw, in a deadly arc of the mouse's fat, furry body.

Mac Flin foresaw it was going to be messy, so he covered his eyes with his hand. "Poor fussy laddie."

WAC! Needlepoint claws connected with the magical amulet, which hung around the mouse's neck, instantly setting off an explosive reaction. The amulet turned into a gleaming white beam that struck the witch's familiar cat named Grim, blasting it into the air because of the magical interaction.

The witch heard the ear-piercing feline scream. Grim landed fur frizzled and trembling. Four paws barely touched the ground before Grim was off again, running as fast as his shaken legs would go, escaping the mouse's powerful explosive beam.

The elves exchanged looks of disbelief and slowly approached the mouse. The silver amulet looked like Onton's.

The mouse held up his silver amulet.

"Onton . . . is that you?" Eppen asked.

The dark elf nodded his reply. Inside, he was screaming, *Yes, I'm Onton, a dark elf! I'm not really a mouse!*

His voice was taken by the witch when she turned him into a mouse.

"That's a powerful magic, your amulet possesses. Are you really Onton?" Eppen questioned the mouse.

There was no time for an answers.

Mac Flin looked up to the witch's green angry eyes boring holes in him.

The leprechaun gulped—red, daggered fingernails pointed at him. Mac Flin gathered all his courage. He'd gotten Onton into this mess, and he was going to get him out.

"Hey, witch, come get me!"

"Ah, but I already have you!"

Her voice snapped like icicles as she bit off each word. "You sneak into my home like mice in the night . . . How foolish!" Her eyes swept each one of them. "What kind of fairies are you? Have you come to steal my fairy light?" She took a step closer.

"She thinks we're fairies," Elfin whispered as they backed up.

"You're afraid . . . Hum, I'll teach you the meaning of fear before we're done."

"Not so fast, witch! I have the book ye want, I'm the leprechaun!"

"You're the one who interfered with my banshee, you stole my book?"

She looked at Onton the mouse.

"Well, your friends have come to what . . ." her laughter was evil, "save you? I think not. I'll have a wonderful time making them glow, then I'll use them—just like my other fairies in my lights. Their size is perfect. I do wonder how they'll help you now?"

Her frosty laugh set Onton the mouse's teeth chittering.

"Enough . . . I'll take my book now, thief," she reached down to pluck the leprechaun from the floor.

The leprechaun was gone, having become invisible.

His disembodied voice taunted, "Yes, I have what ye want, witch!" Mac Flin yelled as loud as he could. Then standing right in front of her, he became visible.

"Aha, I want you, little thief," she screamed, grabbing for him; but again he was inviable.

She whirled in a circle, looking for the leprechaun.

"All right, tricksters, show yourself, or your friends will join the rodent family now!"

Mac Flin materialized right in front of the witch, looking her right in the eye, his voice intense, "You do that, witch, and this wee book," Mac Flin held up the book, "that ye have been after is gone! . . . Are ye up for a bargain, witch?"

"What's your proposal, leprechaun?"

"It's easy, witch—a small trade . . . Change my friend back to an elf, and the book is yours."

The witch had little worry. She'd turn the elf back—what did it matter, she still had all of them. They were now her prisoners.

With a wave of her hand, Witch Lena began chanting . . .

"OR-EE-SHIN, NO LOONGER WILL I SEE YOU AS A MOUSE. EE-DA-MIT-NOW-GET OUT, AND BEGONE FROM THE RODENT SKIN."

Once again, Onton was transformed into an elf.

The spell was reversed; once again Onton was himself.

"Oh, my aching head," the dark elf complained.

Then a sly smile curled his lip as he crept toward the witch. It was the first time he'd been free with company, and he wanted revenge.

Quick as a cat, Witch Lena snatched the small book from the leprechaun. "Aha, finally, I've got both sides of Wizard Galvin's spell book!"

Her hungry smile lasted just moments before the room began to darken. Abruptly, marshmallow clouds began whirlpooling; then from the massing storm, Witch Lena heard . . .

"Lena!"

This witch's eyes widened.

"Wizard Galvin?" she gulped.

"Yes, Lena, that's my girl. You've been a naughty, as I anticipated. Sending a banshee in to Elderwood Forest to get my book of spells . . . Did you really think that would be tolerated? I would never leave my magic behind," the wizard stated. "You, my dear, summoned me, when your greedy hands touched the whole book. Right then I knew you were underfoot. You've just set into motion a new spell—one that binds you to Witchland . . . You're trapped, my dear . . . you might say, by your own hand. Oh, yes, the fairy mist will keep you locked up tight. I believe the fairies have something to discuss with you, I'm sure you'll dislike. Really, my dear, imprisoning fairies, you made a terrible mistake."

The witch knew it was true. If you stumbled into their mystical mist, it would play imaginary tricks on you. One could wander aimlessly lost until a fairy song carried you beyond the mist.

"Let's say, my dear, for a year, that ought to keep you busy . . . Hey, girl."

The room cleared . . . The wizard was gone.

Witch Lena hissed . . .

Lena was so angry.

"How dare that wizard!" she looked down at the leprechaun and grabbed him.

Before he knew it, he was dangling, kicking, and hollering. The witch held him very close to her face. He was afraid she was going to eat him; things were pretty grim.

"You're the cause of this . . . fool. Now you'll pay for your meddling." Her green eyes narrowed. "You'll be settling into a new coat of green, a lean, mean fly-eating machine . . . frog green, hum," she began chanting.

Mac Flin the leprechaun knew he was in deep trouble when the witch began her enchanting spell. And then . . .

A loud crash . . . Witch Lena stopped chanting and swung her head around. Smoke was pouring in, coming from the edges of her large wooden door. Then a loud searing noise, and wood came crashing down . . . Then flames, and her door was incinerated, leaving nothing but a jagged wood frame and charcoaled splinters burning on the ground.

"And a dragon!" the witch screamed. "Now stands were my door should be . . . what else might this dawn bring?"

hank you, Dracolleen, thank you, thank you," Mac Flin sang to himself, while his mind raced to find a solution to his current predicament. He grabbed his waterskin.

"It put us to sleep . . . Maybe it'll work on her."

"O Fairy Queen, please guide this wet nourishment. Lena!" he yelled with all of his might.

Witch Lena whipped back around.

"What?" she yelled right back.

Quick as a cat, the leprechaun heaved his waterskin. Water the companions had gotten from Soul Drinker sloshed in the witch's opened mouth; little dribbled down the witch's chin.

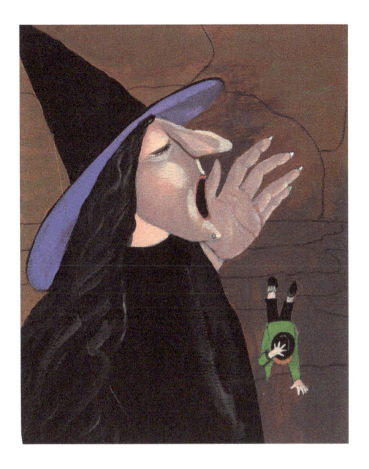

The witch was in shock as she sputtered and swallowed Soul Drinker's liquid elixir. All the time, her eyes never left the leprechaun, and she thought, *I'm going to fix the meddling trickster.*

Next, she closed her eyes, opened her mouth really wide, and yawned—at the same time letting go of the leprechaun.

Mac Flin looked down at the deadly incline and held his breath, for what seemed to be the longest time . . . and thought as he fell through the air, *All I wanted was the shiny dust, I really thought the gold was mine.*

Onton was trying to save the Mac Flin the leprechaun, when he made his spectacular flying leap . . . and . . . tripped . . . landing on top of the witch . . . Suddenly, she began levitating slowly off the floor. Trell reached the fallen leprechaun and heard the witch snore . . . then turned back to his friends.

"Hey, the water spell . . . it's released us, maybe it switched to the snoring witch."

"Onton!" Eppen yelled, "Get off the witch... Let's get out of here!" Leaning far to one side, Onton's expression was one of worry.

"I seem to be stuck, the witch still has me, I fear."

"Maybe our arrows can penetrate her power," Jam yelled.

The three elves shot their magic bolts... Their arrows clattered against an invisible barrier then rebounded off the inside stone tower.

"Her magic, it's so weird," Elfin stated sharply. "We don't have time to understand its power."

Onton was borne along, captured in the witch's levitation, and he wondered how to get out of this terrible situation. As an elf child, the silver amulet burned with power, ready to take control, when the monster tried to eat him; but the elves had been there and killed the troll. The amulet blasted a powerful beam when the jaws of Grim, the witch's familiar, tried to make dinner of him. Now the dark elf leaned close to the witch, with his amulet, which had grown warm in his hand.

He stopped . . . The charm had not saved him when he was a mouse . . . If it didn't work now . . . and awoke the witch instead . . . Suddenly, he was filled with dread. The witch wasn't trying to kill him even though she'd turned him into a rodent. Maybe it only worked when his life is threatened—was that the difference? . . . Could it be? He pressed his charm onto the witch . . . In a sudden magical surge, Onton was thrown free.

As air seeping out of a balloon, the witch was blasted upward; then she began shrinking and spiraled down, to where she lay sleeping curled upon the ground.

"Oh, my aching head," Mac Flin moaned, looking at the shrinking witch with dread. "She would have turned me into a frog, if the dragon hadn't burned her door like a log."

Dracolleen the dragon was happy once more, finally being reunited with Onton when she blazed through the witch's door. Pinpoints of lights blinked in a blue mist that snaked across the floor, and fairies revealed themselves, as they flew in by the score. In a song, they began their dance of magic, against the witch's spell that held their friends against their will. With hands held tight, using all their might, the glass melted away. The captive fairies made their escape, just as when Lena awoke, flying right past her, with their lights still growing bright.

Grim turned loose.

"It's Witch Lena, can't you see, it's me!"

Grim, her cat, looked her right in the eye. "I TOLD YOU, IT WAS A TRAP! BUT YOU NEVER LISTEN TO ME," was all Grim would say.

"Let's be on our way," Eppen called out, "while her hands are still busy with her familiar Grim."

They stepped through the burned-out door, into soppy fog.

"Where to?" Jam asked. "Which way from here?"

Then from the hazy dew, a fairy flew into view.

"Lady of the light!" Trell breathed. It was love at first sight. "You're our size, how can it be?"

"Here in our land of enchantment, we're whatever we wish to be. With all your help, we were able to pass the witch and free our captive friends. We thank you all. You are very brave, Dracolleen. The day will come, you'll be full grown, and the witch will shutter in fear when she hears your name. Trell, this whistle is a gift. Its song will reach us, if ever we can help. My name is Bree. I will be your guide to Elderwood, if you'll just follow me."

So it was. On that mist-driven day, the good fairy led the companions away, past barbed-filled ravine they moved, through the land of In Between where fairy can always be seen, and then on to Elderwood Forest. Trell smiled and touched his cheek. The kiss he received from Bree, in memory he would always keep.

Family Album

KW Limited Fantasy Creation

ABOUT THE AUTHOR

Kathryn May Howard Whitaker was born in Los Angeles, California, on January 20, 1941. Her exceptional talent was evidenced in the fact that she was a self-taught artist and contributed beautiful works of art in numerous genres. In addition to being portrait artist and sculptor, she painted watercolor, oils, pastels, and pen and ink. Mrs. Whitaker could mix any color just by looking at it and would try any medium until she had conquered it. She made her own molds for elves and leaf fairies, and she painted a fresco of the cresol horse. To round out her talent and versatility, she authored and illustrated two (as yet, unpublished) books.

Mrs. Whitaker started the Art Guild in Carver, Massachusetts, in 1979. She succeeded in capturing the charm of, and her love for, New England in her beautiful paintings. She resided in New England for forty-five years and recreated the shorelines of New England from Connecticut to Maine. As a teacher, she shared all her knowledge of the arts with students; she felt strongly that teachers should share all there is to know.

Her work was found in many gift shops and galleries in Plymouth, Massachusetts, and one of her prints of Plymouth Harbor and Wharf is owned by the late Ronald Reagan. The original oil paintings of *America's Home Town and Town Wharf-Plymouth Harbor* are going to hang in the Plymouth Town hall in Plymouth, Massachusetts. These works, and other information, can be found at http://kathrynwhitaker.com/art work prints.html and http://www.legacy.com/orbituaries/wickedlocal-plymouth/obituary.aspx?n=kathryn-whitaker&pid=172756202.

Mrs. Whitaker passed away on October 1, 2014, leaving her astonishing legacy and volume of beautiful works for the world to enjoy.

CPSIA information can be obtained
at www.ICGtesting.com
Printed in the USA
BVHW02*0710090518
515692BV00001B/1/P